Just a Passing Phrase III

Mary Easty

Collated by Richard Easty

Contents

Annie Says

Annie's nephew is getting a bit cheeky — she hopes it's just a passing phrase.

Singing Kettle

At the foot of the Milham Hills, on the south road, there is a tea room called "the Singing Kettle". It has stood there since the 1920s, when Thomas Badger, a baker from Bartford, rented a barn from a local farmer so that he could expand his business. Badgers' cakes were so delicious that the new shop became very popular, and within a few months Thomas built a satellite bakery behind the barn and brought in some of his finest confectioners. Soon the barn was turned into a pretty tea-room, and as its fame spread, satisfied customers gave it its name.

Thomas Badger's family ran the tea room, and the kettle sang from morning till early evening, as his daughters served "mixed fancies" on flowered dishes. Badgers were famous for their cream horns, eclairs, chocolate boxes, maids of honour, jam puffs, iced fondants, doughnuts, cherry buns... and many, many more as they say today, which flowed in from the bakery and out onto the welcoming plates in no time. Thomas fenced-off a car park and added extra tables and even built living accommodation next to the tea room, and the family moved in. The Singing Kettle was a great success.

Unfortunately, this could not last forever. The war years took their toll, and although afterwards business improved, there were difficulties. The old couple died and their two grand-daughters, Rose and Emily, were themselves getting older. Costs were high, and they could not afford to employ staff. The Singing Kettle hit hard times, and the sisters thought they might have to give in, and close down.

Then a strange coincidence occurred. A letter arrived from the governor of the prison at Birmingham. His astonishing news was that one of his prisoners, whose name was John Badger, was due for release, and had no relative willing to take him in. It had been established that he was a distant cousin, and the request was that the sisters would allow him to stay with them, even for a very short time, until accommodation could be provided for him elsewhere. Rent would be provided, and supervision by a local officer. Somewhat overwhelmed, Rose and Emily decided to agree. They made up the spare room bed, and within a few days a police car drew into the car park, discharged a passenger and drove away quickly.

John Badger was tall and thin, with a pale face and a sparse black beard. The cousins stared at each other; then Rose and Emily welcomed him in with old-fashioned courtesy and Singing Kettle cakes. John began to think he had died and gone to heaven, which had always seemed unlikely. Over the next few weeks, he made himself useful, painting the tea-room, cleaning the bakery, clearing the overgrown car park, and having a good look around. Neighbours and passing motorists noticed the improvements, and when John exhumed the old signpost, they began to show interest. Rose and Emily reopened the bakery, got a few people in to help, and visitors started to call for tea.

John had his own ideas too. He made calls on his mobile to some old friends from Birmingham, and they came down from town to see him. They helped him to build an annexe onto the bakery, and drove up at all hours to work there with him. When Rose and Emily questioned him, he said he had a wonderful business plan which would add to their profits. The Singing Kettle was so busy they had little time to bother about him. His "rent" was useful, and he went every Tuesday to town, as he said he had promised. John's friends brought machinery into the annexe, and installed lights that were kept on all night. John put up heavy curtains; as he said, no point in wasting electricity.

Then John bought an Ice Cream van which he decorated with slogans, "Badger's Ice" was one, "Happy Cake" and "Special Coke". Rose and Emily had the bakery going well by now, and supplied John with trays of their best delicacies, and he set them out for all to see and drove round the nearby towns and villages, always returning with an empty van and plenty of money to share.

News travelled fast and far, the Singing Kettle's re-found fame even spread overseas. It seemed that visitors of all colours, races and genders turned up to enjoy cakes in the barn and a trip to the annexe. The mayor of Bartford heard of the success and came to call. As the mayoral car rolled in to the car park, John proudly introduced him to a guest who happened to be in the tea room - the mayor of Bogota! They shook hands with great enthusiasm, and before they left, had discussed twinning the two towns, and exchanged addresses.

Success built on success, and by the end of the summer, the Singing Kettle had picked up to the pre-war levels again. The Ice Cream cart was cheered into each local village and returned empty to the tea-room every evening.

I was there one afternoon, enjoying a baba-au-rhum in the tea room, washed down with a special coffee from the annexe, when two uniformed policemen walked in; the local constable from Bartford and his comrade from Lionbury. They looked round the room, and quite a few of our foreign visitors froze. The café was busy, but Rose and Emily showed them to a table in the centre of the room, and continued with their work, passing plates, taking orders, placid smiles on their faces.

3

Then the van turned in to the car park. "Oh, look!" said our local bobby. "The Ice Man cometh!" He turned to his companion, "I'll introduce you to him."

"Hi, there," he called to John, smiling broadly. "We meet at last! Been wanting to meet you for quite some time." The two officers moved forward. Chaos ensued. Rose dropped her huge plate of cream puffs just behind them, and as PC Bartford slid about amongst them, unfortunately the meringue Emily was holding out with her tongs was squashed into PC Lionbury's face. The customers screamed and ran about, and amongst the confusion the van roared off towards the hills, its chimes still ringing out as it disappeared .

Well, the kettle is still singing, though the customers are not quite so many or so merry now. People still call and ask for the Specials and seem surprised to be handed the table d'hote. Emily and Rose miss the fun, but life goes on.

Annie Says

Annie thinks the police will soon catch the neighbourhood burglar. "He's been in so many houses," she says, "they must have a complete set of his fingernails by now".

Slow Day

Charlie always wakes at daybreak. When he was a child it was his father clattering down the stairs on his way to The Works, then later his brothers in their heavy boots, then himself rushing off.

He had done the best of them all, in charge of the engine that controlled The Works - always kept it in tip-top form, orderly, neat and tidy, same as he still likes everything today. As soon as he opens his eyes, he pulls his armchair up close to the window. He sleeps all night in the chair, but nobody needs to know: it's warm and comfortable and it saves time. Time is important now.

He leans forward to catch the first light as it approaches across the gardens opposite his flat, streaking the black sky with pale stripes. The thrush at the top of the hawthorn tree mutters and flutters and then celebrates the new day with shrill song. Familiar outlines appear as the ground-mist rises, and colours become clearer, grey grass becomes green, grey roofs glint silver, grey walls glow redder. Other birds join in the chorus. He watches intently, savouring the familiar moments. Charlie focuses on the lane nearby, watching the cats as they return home under the hedges, along the walls, over the gates and through the cat-flaps for breakfast.

The first human figure is always the newsagent, Bob, up and out to his shop to take in the papers. Bob is getting older, too, Charlie thinks, and he smiles in sympathy at the slight stoop, the slower stride. Bob glances up at the window and gives a stiff salute. Charlie's eyes never move from the view, as his fingers fumble on the window-sill for his cigarettes. Before he can open the packet he sees the milkman's van turn into the road. Every morning Charlie shakes his head at the sight, remembering the old days when the cart called at every house and the horse would wait patiently as the pints were delivered at a run.

The light is changing now, and Charlie narrows his eyes as the sun begins to show over the chimney-tops. He glances at the clock on his mantelpiece - a present from The Works when he retired, its own little engine beating away in its glass case - still very early, but he knows where to look next. He turns a little and stares towards the top road, and there it comes, the hospital bus bringing in the day-shift of nurses, cleaners, porters. It will soon drop its passengers and reload with the tired night-staff, passing again in the other direction. All is going to plan, as always.

Charlie leans back more comfortably, takes a cigarette out of the packet and puts it between his lips, but just as be opens the box of matches there is a little flurry of activity. He is all attention again as one of his favourite moments unrolls before him - the paper-boys appear, seemingly from every direction, in ones and twos, some running, some on bikes. Some of the lads know Charlie and wave as they go past, but he is too slow to respond and they never see the answering hand and the smile. However, the smile remains. The cogs are all turning, Charlie's morning is moving along smoothly.

Another bus passes the top of the road, and another going the other way, early workers off to shops and offices, factories and workshops. More pedestrians are about, and Charlie recognises many of them. He knows the regulars, those who walk quickly with heads down - "on the minutes," he thinks to himself - or those who have time to wait for friends and chat as they go. Any minute now he will see the schoolboys, ties already askew, shoes in need of a bit of blacking, the giggling, gossiping girls in their bright jackets, and hurrying mothers with pushchairs delivering small children to their nurseries.

Charlie feels part of the morning, as he watches the world unfold before his eyes. The engine is awake, the machine is running smoothly, wheels are turning. He lights his cigarette at last and leans deep into the cushions. Someone will bring his dinner, make him a cup of tea... He can relax and doze now, his duty complete until the next dawn.

Annie Says

Annie is so sorry to hear of the TV star who is HGV positive.

A Wedding

I parked my car at the bottom of the hill and glanced at my watch. Plenty of time to read her letter again-though I already knew it off by heart. "Dear Auntie Catherine," it said, "thank you so much for the wonderful wedding present. You have always been so generous to me, the one person who never forgets my birthday, and I can't believe I have never seen you! Mother says you were there when I was born, but of course I can't remember that, and I have her name and yours too, Sarah Catherine. I have the photograph of you at Mother's wedding, the little sister, who was her bridesmaid, as Amy will be mine. I do wish you could be well enough to come to my wedding! Please, please try, it would make me so happy if you were with me just this once." As I read, the bells began to ring, calling everyone to the service.

Time to move on, I thought. Hastily stuffing the paper into my pocket I locked the car and followed the familiar winding path up the hill. Everyone who had ever lived in the village knew this hill, where the young people walked when we were courting. . . an old fashioned word I had not heard nor spoken for many a long year, I realised, smiling. . . a very special place, full of memories.

The slopes seemed steeper than I had expected, but near the top I searched for a grassy hollow that I remembered, sheltered from the breeze, and sat down to watch the scene that stretched out below. I could see our old schoolhouse, the rows of shops and cottages, and in the distance the farm where we had lived, the fields where we had played. In front of the church was an open space, full of friends waiting for the bride to arrive.

The bells rang out a welcome as two cars drew into the square, and I leaned forward, unseen.

Out of the first car came a tall woman, wearing a huge white hat with flowers pinned round the crown. I smiled: my sister looked just like our mother had looked at Sal's own wedding. With her was the young bridesmaid in a long blue frock. This must be Amy! I caught my breath... I knew how proud she was feeling on this happy day.

Much jostling now among the crowd, as the second car arrived. First, Sal's husband Tom. I could hardly bring myself to look at him. The old terror struck me for a moment. He had not changed since the last time I saw him. Tall straight, red-faced, cold, hard, eyes. "I'll agree to this," I could hear his words as if he was spitting them out at me again "only to please Sal. She is a good woman; wants to help you as a good woman would. We'll take care of your child, but only on condition we never see you again." I kept my part of the bargain, I thought, and no one will ever know how hard it has been.

I brushed tears from my face as I strained to watch the car door open again, and a glowing young woman in a fairytale frock took his arm. I stood, unable to move, astonished as I stared at myself, twenty years ago... then the moment passed. The bells were silent, the breeze blew the sound of organ music and happy voices up the hill towards me. The square below was empty. I turned and walked back to my car.

A Tale of Our Times

John Robertson was really pleased when he heard that the Inspectors would be coming to the school on one of his days as a Volunteer. He was attached to young Jenny Andrews' class; there were many children among the new intake of eleven and twelve-year olds who needed extra attention, specially in reading, and he loved his role. A widower, his own family long grown-up, he cherished the close contacts and interesting new experiences. At present he was mentoring two children, each with individual difficulties but equally in need of the attention not available to them at school or at home. Having the same pupils several times a week helped John to build up a trusting and friendly relationship with each one, and Miss Andrews found his support invaluable.

In "real life," as he put it, John was the Rector of an inner-city parish, and most of his contacts were with older people, the parish council, the various groups and clubs which met in the church hall. Working with the schoolchildren was a pleasant new interest for him, and he was diligent and meticulous.

The school was well-prepared for the Inspection. All was going swimmingly when Mrs. Diggle, the Head, brought the visitors into Jenny's room and introduced them. Mr. Barlow settled down to watch Jenny's lesson and Mrs. Kyle came across to sit by John.

"And your name is?" she asked John's pupil.

"Sammy," said the child. John noticed the cool appraising look on Mrs. Kyle's face, and Sammy's uncomfortable wriggle in response. He so much wanted the little girl to do herself justice. In their weeks together they were beginning to build a bond of mutual respect and equal effort, which might be difficult to demonstrate. Sammy too wanted to do her best for her teacher.

John worked hard to put Sammy at her ease, and eventually she was able to ignore the visitor and her confidence improved enough for her to manage quite a fluent passage. "Well done, Sam!" he praised her, and even Mrs. Kyle defrosted a little. Sam however was so relieved that she leapt out of her seat and threw her arms round John's neck. "I didn't know I could read that!"she exulted, as John patted her arm and gently eased her back into her chair. Mrs. Kyle's expression changed and her face hardened.

At that moment the bell rang . The class was dismissed for lunch and Mrs. Diggle returned for the guests.

Mr. Barlow was all smiles and compliments. Mrs. Kyle however was pale and stern. "I have to say, Mrs. Diggle", she began, "I am most concerned about the incident I have just observed with my own eyes in this Mentor's interaction with his pupil. Most distressing and disturbing". The teachers turned to John in astonishment. His face was crimson "An incident?" he queried. Mrs. Kyle looked him squarely in the eye. "I distinctly saw the young girl embrace you, which you did nothing to discourage, and I may say appeared to enjoy, and you yourself most inappropriately touched her."

There was complete silence, broken by Mrs. Diggle. "Mr. Robertson?" she prompted. John was so horrified, mortified, that he could hardly speak. "I really can't understand your interpretation of the child's perfectly natural, spontaneous reaction", he spluttered. Mrs. Kyle looked smug. "So you can't deny what I saw?" she said.

Mrs. Diggle took over. "Reverend Robertson," she said,

emphasising the title, "you know that your colleagues and I hold you in the utmost respect in this school, and have never had any cause to doubt you. I would like you now to take time to write your own detailed description of this interaction which seems to have so much alarmed the Inspector. Please leave your response in my room, then return home. I will contact you as soon as possible."

Jenny was crying openly. "This is ridiculous," she said. "Mr. Robertson is such a help to us all, and the children love him." "So it would seem," said the Inspector drily, sweeping out of the room. "The parents must be informed immediately," they heard her say.

"I'll help you to write the paper," Jenny tried to comfort John. "Just explain what happened. Things like this go on all the time when deprived children find someone who cares about them."

John picked up his things and walked slowly home, so shocked that he could not think clearly. Perhaps he had encouraged the children in the wrong way? Been a negative influence on them?

His daughter Jane phoned later. "How did the Inspection go, Dad?" she asked "Fairly well, at first," he began, but she interrupted. "Oh, that's great!" she said. "We're just dashing out now. Talk to you soon!" and she was off.

He looked round at his study. No one to tell. Nobody wanted to know. John walked across the rectory garden to the church. It was getting dark now but he only switched on a couple of lights — he knew every inch of this lovely old place. Sitting down heavily on a pew near the front he tried to pray. The words were almost impossible to find. As he prepared to leave, he heard voices outside. Boys playing in the graveyard, he thought. Then he heard the words — paedo! pervert! which

12

at first he could not make out. When they became clearer he hurried home.

Later, the phone rang again. "Reverend Robertson" the answerphone announced for him. A harsh voice shrieked at him. "Oh, I know who you are, Reverend, and now I know what you are, too! My Sammy didn't know how to tell me what you had been up to!" The voice was quieter now and more menacing. "An innocent child! Taking advantage! Good thing that woman spotted you!" Now the tone changed to sneers. "Lost your little job, didn't you! Sent home from school! Well" — voice rising again — "you'll regret this. After all the years of love and care she's had from us! I'm her mother, you'd better remember that! We'll have every penny you've got, make sure this doesn't happen to any other loving family..." The threats went on. John put the phone back on its rest and his head in his hands.

That was the night the first stones broke his study window — Kristallnacht John thought. Night after night, lads crept in and damaged his rooms, wrecked his garden, stole his computer, damaged his books. Stained glass in the church was shattered, gravestones overturned. Danger seemed to be closing in on him; mocking voices calling from the darkness, insults on the phone, threatening letters too. He called a colleague to take the Sunday services for him. Apparently the congregation was larger than usual.

One morning he found the police at his door. Henry Vaughan was one of his parishoners, solid in his support. The woman constable avoided his eyes. Henry was businesslike, recording a formal complaint from Sammy's family. John gave a statement, had his fingerprints taken.

That night John had another telephone call. He was horrified to hear a hysterical Sammy sobbing. "I'm sorry, Sir, I'm so sorry! Me Mam's give me a hiding 'cos I didn't tell about the lady. When are you coming back, Sir?"Without speaking, John replaced the receiver.

Next morning, Mrs. Diggle and Jenny arrived, with a solicitor. John feared the worst and opened the door most unwillingly. There was good news, however – case dismissed. So many people who knew John well and respected him had spoken for him. "So glad, John" said Mrs. Diggle, and Jenny gave him a hug. "So, it's all over, Sir," said the solicitor. John made them coffee, and saw them off. "It's all over," he repeated to himself.

Then he looked round his outraged house, broken, slashed, defiled. He saw himself in the mirror, hair wild, face thin and lined, clothes creased and dirty. He walked across the garden to the church and went in. Graffiti on the door, coloured glass on the altar, hymn books scattered and torn. He knelt to pray, then straightened up. He walked through the gate without looking back. "It's all over", he thought.

Jane rang several times but got no answer, and went abroad on holiday. Mrs. Diggle called once or twice, and Jenny and her boyfriend called with an invitation to their wedding, but the door was locked. A little girl searched the woods and haunted the graveyard all through the summer.

Annie Says

Annie loves street parties.
She never misses the Moss Side Carnivore.

Works Experience

"Hello, love!"

She looked up from her baking, astonished to see him.

"Home so early?" she asked. Then "What's happened?" as she noticed the state he was in.

He waited at the shadowy door, not moving, and she stood up. "Just look at you !" she grumbled. "Covered in dust and dirt! Plaster and bits of brick! Don't come in on the clean floor!" but her voice faded as she looked at him more closely. "Something's wrong - has there been an accident?"

He nodded, and took a step towards her, where pale sunlight shone through the kitchen window. She saw the strained face, the taut expression. "Oh, Dan - are people hurt?"

"Too many," he replied, almost in a whisper.

"None - killed?" She clutched her apron, hardly daring to listen to the answer. Theirs was a close community, all the men and boys employed at the Works, and many of the women too. Dan was here in the room with her, but what about the others?

Instead of answering, he turned away and looked out through the doorway. His gaze fastened first on the porch, where his cap hung on its peg, his bike leaned against the post. He looked slowly up the path into the little garden, at the flowers she had planted and the vegetables he had tended. He raised his eyes past the brick wall he had built, and up to the hills high above the chimneys of the Works, and then turned back to answer her question.

"Too many," he said again, very sadly.

As he spoke, the Works hooter began to blow the signal for a disaster, one long mournful tone followed by two short ones, repeated over and over.

15

She steadied herself on the scrubbed tabletop and bent to take off her apron, ready to run with him to the scene. When she looked up he had gone, and coming down the path she saw five men slowly approaching the cottage, carrying a covered stretcher.

Annie Says

My friend Annie has been noticing how long the window-cleaner spends across the road. "I may not be Jekyll and Hyde," she said, "but I know what's going on there!"

Larry Weller: A Sad Story

Propping himself up against the kitchen door, he emptied the pockets. A half-empty cigarette packet, a scratched lighter, crumpled handkerchief, bits of paper, all placed quietly on the table. Cheap pens, tickets, receipts, nothing to identify the owner. No money, no mobile phone — he puffed out his cheeks with relief. No immediate problems, then. Nothing he had to do now. And his own wallet safely stashed away as usual in his trouser pocket. He swept the collection into a tea towel and rolled it up behind the microwave, his head pounding.

He had to admit he was not up to nights like this. Not any more! A few years ago he would have been up for it! Meetings of the ex-area managers at the Grand Hotel, best in the city, meal, a few drinks—par for the course before he was "ex", before he retired he would have gone on till dawn! But tonight... so hot, stuffy, noisy; Larry felt quite sorry for himself. Most of the others had gone out on the town, clubbing, and he had slunk off home. Luckily somebody had pushed him into a cab and paid his fare, as he had done before for others. Now he had only to face Clarice — in the morning, he hoped. Steadying himself on all fours, he climbed up the stairs, avoiding the ones that creaked, carefully, slowly, quietly, and slipped into bed.

"What time d'you call this?" the inevitable furious whisper. Nobody wanted to wake Gran. But he seemed already asleep and Clarice turned over with a thump.

An hour or two later the phone rang.

Larry was still flat out. Clarice answered. "D'you know it's four o'clock in the morning?" "May I speak to Mr. Larry

Webber?"

"Who's speaking?"

"This is the Bunny Club," said the voice. "We have his jacket here."

"You've got WHAT!" she was out of bed now, fury burning like a halo surrounding her.

"For you, I think," she snarled.

Larry turned over and looked out of one eye.

Gran appeared at the bedroom door. "Is it the police?" she asked hopefully. "Not yet," came the reply.

Clarice rammed the phone into Larry's shaky hand and led Gran back to her room. Larry stammered into the receiver but it had gone off.

After some discussion they decided on a cup of tea, followed by Gran, who never missed anything. Clarice soon pounced on the little bundle and laid it out for inspection. "Thought you'd stopped smoking", she scoffed, lifting up the packet with outstretched fingertips and dropping it into the waste basket. "And this rubbish!" adding the lighter. As she sifted through the papers, the phone rang again. There was a tussle, as Larry, dreading what might happen next, leapt up.

"Hi, Laz!" the loud, jovial voice made Larry's face contort in pain. It was Dave, one of the other ex-managers. "You missed a treat last night, lad! Great time! You should have stayed a bit longer!"

Clarice and Gran were listening intently to the tinny tones. Gran turned up her hearing aid.

"We went to the Ritz and the Three Stars and ended up, you'll never guess, at the Bunny! Never seen anything like it, anyway, not for years, eh!" Clarice and Gran drew in their breath and concentrated again "Well", and here Dave's voice dropped a decibel or two, "I need you to do something for me. I'm in a fine mess if you don't, Li. Remember, I helped you into a cab last night outside the Grand! Well, I've gone and left my jacket at the Bunny! Can you go and get it for me? It's very like yours, brown Harris tweed, you'll know it when you see it. And, Li, don't let Clarice find out! She might tell Marge, there'd be hell to pay!"

Annie Says

Annie watches the Antiques Road Show. She has some antiques herself in the family, passed down from limb to limb.

The Cherry Tree

Julia watched the dawn break, and the early light begin to touch her cherry tree. It was about to show the signs of early blossom, the tightly-curled buds open just enough to promise the pure white petals clasped inside. Julia loved the tree, it had mirrored the moments of her life. As a child, she had climbed up with her brothers to hide amongst its branches, smiled with her new husband on their wedding day as the flowers fell like confetti around them. Their children had slept in their prams in its shade, and later had played safely on the swing hanging from its sturdy arms. The cherry tree had grown to maturity as she had, a symbol for her of life and continuity.

A cloud shadowed the view, and Julia turned, wincing as she moved. The pain in her side increased; today she must face her appointment at the hospital. She feared she already knew what the outcome would be. Slowly she stretched her feet to the floor and put on her dressing-gown.

The spring was soon over, the blossom fallen and the tree dressed in its green cloak. Julia's bed had been pushed nearer to the window now, and she stared out unhappily, unable to smile at the antics of the squabbling blackbirds and mischievous squirrels. The bouts of sickness, side-effects of her treatment, left her tired and weak.

Even the beloved tree was no comfort. She hardly noticed as the leaves turned crimson and then brown, blowing about in useless protest against the rising winds. The birds gathering on the emptying branches were preparing to fly south, leaving few signs of life in the deserted garden.

As the year wore on, the family became more and more worried. The doctors came and spent a long time in Julia's room. She was too frail to say much to them, preferring to turn her head towards the window. She stared almost unseeingly at the cherry tree, which itself looked barely alive, a stark silhouette against the darkening skies. Downstairs, Julia's family asked anxious questions, and were surprised at the reply.

"The treatment has in fact worked," they were told. "It is up to her now, there is nothing more we can do - you must help her to hold on: if she can survive until the Spring, she will surely pull through."

"How can we help her?" they asked in concern.

Winter was in charge, cold, grey, colourless days, no hint of returning life outside. They were taking turns to sit with her now, day and night, holding her hand whilst she slept, talking softly to her when she woke, trying to encourage her to rally. "If only the tree could give her strength," they thought.

Towards morning, one grand-daughter came to Julia's room to replace another. Shivering a little as she pulled a jersey round her shoulders, she walked to the window and looked out. She stared, unbelievingly, at the cherry tree as the moonlight picked it out, and for a moment thought a miracle had caused it to blossom. The branches glistened, loaded with silver flowers - of snow!

"Snow!!" At the exclamation, Julia stirred and woke. They surrounded her with warm shawls and lifted her head a little to look outside, crying "See! your tree!"

At first, Julia was blank - then suddenly, relaxed and smiled. The girls hugged each other and kissed her. In the morning the blue sky beamed through the tracery, but the air was icy and the illusion held.

By the end of the day the snow began to melt - but the tree had done its work and Julia had turned the corner.

All in the Mind

Telephone lines were bouncing, computers flashing, messages flying round the country like lightning, and, like lightning, the impact was very mixed. "Friends Re-united" was the hackneyed headline, "class of" whatever, "50-year anniversary". At some breakfast tables faces lit up. At others, hearts sank. In response, some sent apologies, some didn't acknowledge the invitation at all. But quite a lot accepted, even for "self and partner". The organisers, former head girl Brenda and her husband former head boy Norman, were pleasantly surprised.

Caterers and a marquee were arranged, the school band bribed with individual performance fees. Former staff from fifty years ago were (optimistically) contacted, but few of them admitted to being still alive, even fewer agreed to attend, and all of them defaulted on the day except for one, Miss Pegg. This lady lived some miles from the school, the one teacher everyone remembered for her maths lessons, which she had managed to make both terrifying and also great fun. Even at over ninety years of age she was completely independent and was the first to arrive on the day, driving her own car. Brenda and Norman stood on the porch steps with Miss Pegg between them, greeting everyone warmly. At first they were slightly taken aback, as a crowd of unrecognisable elderly men and women approached up the drive to shake their hands. Luckily, Miss Pegg usually came to the rescue... "Hello, Freda, how's your sister?" or "Well, John, back from Abu Dhabi, then!" and they all knew her at once. Dear Miss Pegg!

Norman noticed that the biggest and flashiest cars were parked prominently on the drive, whilst smaller, dirtier ones hid away behind the bicycle sheds. Brenda smiled as drinks circulated in the hot sunshine and the voices grew louder and less guarded. The grounds were soon filled with chatter as old friends were "re-united."

The men talked to each other about cars, football, their golf-handicaps and, where points could be scored, the jobs they had had before retirement. The women discussed their families, high-flying children and grand-children, foreign holidays and busy social lives, at the same time unobtrusively inspecting each others' clothes, hair styles, tans, accents... Old memories dredged-up, carefully censored, quickly dropped.

Miss Pegg moved around, with some difficulty on her two sticks, from group tp group, helping to keep the conversation flowing. The refreshment tent filled and emptied, the drinks ran out, the band played, was paid and departed. Endless photographs were taken, cameras compared. A very few addresses, phone or email numbers were exchanged. As evening approached, people began to drift away.

Brenda and Norman had to wait for the marquee to be taken down. They sat, suddenly exhausted, on the steps, and Miss Pegg waited with them. "How did it go?" they prompted her. "It was very good," she said. "You did very well."

"Didn't some of them look OLD!" Norman seemed really surprised. Brenda joined in "and the clothes (smoothing her smart skirt) — nearly everyone with grey hair, except for the fashionable ones", she added, conscious of her own glowing auburn rinse. "You seemed to recognise everybody!" turning to Miss Pegg. "Not at first", Miss Pegg admitted, "but once we began to reminisce, things came back," and she smiled. What things? Brenda wondered.

"Some of the men had really let themselves go," said

Norman. "Don't take enough exercise, no energy. Of course, we're lucky, being so well and healthy. That's what keeps us young, I expect." Brenda remembered a phrase she had heard. "A man is as young as he feels," she said, looking approvingly at her husband, "and a woman is as young as she looks. There's a lot in that, isn't there?" she asked Miss Pegg, glancing at her own reflection in the glass doorway.

"Here come the porters," said Miss Pegg, pulling herself up from the chair. As she walked to her car, Brenda and Norman on each side, she added "My father had a similar saying. It made us children laugh, but there may be something to learn from it. It went 'Oh would some power the giftie gie us, to see ourselves as others see us.' Scottish, I think."

As they waved her off, Norman said "Poor old thing! Didn't know what she was on about most of the time, did she?" "She must be very tired," Brenda agreed "She does very well for her age."

Annie Says

Cheer up, is Annie's motto,
it's never too late to say die.

A Little Surprise

Oh, good! I thought, a letter, not a bill.

I sliced open the envelope with my buttery knife, licked my fingers and sat down to read. Immediately, something about the letter frightened me. I began to feel cold, uncomfortable, my head filled with strange sounds.

I skimmed the words that jumped out at me: "your name on my list" — "new legislation" — "chance to discover your ancestors" — "who is in your family tree?" — "letter of application" — "signed, Sandra P. Hackett." I remembered the comics my brothers had shared: Shock! Horror! and a huge fist lunging out of the square. I folded the paper into my apron pocket.

In a few minutes I remembered where I was, and looked for reassurance round the room we still called the parlour. These had been my safe and happy walls all my life, "my Mam's house" to all of us but especially to me, the youngest of seven and the last to stay on after she died. I looked across at the chair by the fireplace and smiled at her shadow.

I had been born as we all had in the house next door where my grandparents had lived. My dad had been called up "for a soldier" when the war started and my Mam had been glad of their help for there were already six of us. Dad had been badly wounded in the very first fighting, and sent home. I arrived soon after, their little surprise, they always called me, and I must have been a surprise, too! Our Jenny was already eight, and then there were our boys, my four big brothers, Alan, Dennis, Fred and Billy, and the oldest girl Doffy, christened Dorothy after my gran, just sixteen when I was born. All us girls, Doffy and Jenny and my Mam and me, we all had the same fuzzy blond hair, long and wild like a huge bonnet.

Our dad died soon after I arrived and I don't remember him really, just big and quiet, but our Mam kept us all going – loud and funny, always laughing. Our boys didn't always go to school when they should, and our Mam often had to hide from the school-board man, but it didn't do any harm and they all grew up strong and stocky and lived round about, in and out of the house with their own small children. Doffy left school early and got work, always changing her job, but she was lively like Mam and liked to be off and out, dressed up to go dancing. She was only eighteen when she sailed off to America, one of the first GI brides. I only just remember her as she was then, bright and sparkling like Mam, but very soon she came back again and exchanged her GI for a local man and settled in the city. Sadly our Jenny died when she was only a little girl, appendix they told us, that could be cured now. So the "little surprise" was all Mam had left at home, and I stayed with her till she died and the place was mine. And suddenly, this extraordinary letter had jolted me out of my safe, ordinary life.

I looked at it over and over that day. When I had made my bed I sat on the faded counterpane and read it word by word. I smoothed it out again when I stopped for a cup of tea as the washer swirled. I propped it up against the milk jug whilst my egg boiled at dinner time. I carried it in my purse when I hurried out for a loaf, fingering it nervously as I put away the change. I even took it up to bed with me and examined it before I put out the light. And every time I looked at it, I heard those muttering voices in my head, that I had always heard when strange things happened. . . I remember it even when I was very small, sitting in my pram as Mam pushed me quickly past the women outside the shops, the

26

women watching slyly, talking about us as we hurried by. The first day at school when the teachers were asking Mam about me, and I heard it when people asked me questions I couldn't understand, uncomfortable, a warning to take care. I heard it now, rumbling like distant thunder, be careful it said, about something you will never know. At last I fell asleep.

By morning I had decided what to do. I dusted Mam's chair and laid the letter in its envelope on her pink cushion. And then I looked in Mam's notebook for Doffy's phone number and dialled it. I couldn't ask Mam for advice, I reasoned, nor discuss it with our boys of course, so Doffy was all I had.

After the usual hallos, apologies for not keeping in touch more often, inquiries about health and families, I read out the letter. Doffy was silent, as astounded as I was! "What are you going to do?" she kept asking. "What should I do?" I wanted to know. Doffy seemed really shocked. "I can't understand what they want," I told her. "Who is this woman, anyway? What has our family history got to do with her?" We both talked, often at the same time and saying the same things. The voices began again, very quietly in the background.

Then "It must all be a stupid mistake," she said shakily. "Don't worry about it. Mam wouldn't want us to look back." She was getting upset, and I was too, and we were both crying. But this was exactly the advice I wanted to hear, the best possible way to handle this whole silly business. The voices stopped. "You're right," I said. "Thanks so much, Doffy — I'll forget the whole thing. I don't want this at my age."

"Who does Sandra P. Hackett think she is, anyway?" cried my sister hysterically. "Nosy beggar!" I sobbed, and we were off, back on old terms, laughing and shrieking.

"What would Mam have said?" I howled

"I know!" hiccupped Doffy, "she would have screamed like us!"

"I'm going to show Sandra P. Hackett what I think about her letter of application," I sniffed, wiping my eyes, and I shuffled across to Mam's chair, picked up the envelope between two fingers and dropped it on the fire.

As the paper burned brightly, I looked again at the chair. Mam's shadow nodded approvingly and I heard her laugh.

Annie Says

It's time, Annie thinks, that the government cramped down on these gangs of federal youths.